TOFU TaKES TiME

by Helen H. Wu
illustrated by Julie Jarema

beaming books
MINNEAPOLIS

Today I'm making tofu with NaiNai. All from scratch!
"Let's see if you are patient enough to make tofu,"
NaiNai says, rinsing soybeans into a big bowl.

PLINK

PLANK

PLUNK

"That doesn't look like tofu!" I say. "It looks like seeds."
"You're right! Making tofu takes time," NaiNai says.

And it takes seeds from soil, rain, and the sunshine.

NaiNai blends the soybeans with water.

CLICK

CLACK

WHIRRRR

"NaiNai, is it ready yet?" I ask.

"Not yet," NaiNai says.
"Remember that tofu takes
time. And patience."

And it takes some water, from river and creek.

We strain the soy milk through cheesecloth into a pot.

PITTER

PITTER

PATTER

"It takes so long," I say. "Why don't we buy tofu from the supermarket?"

"Lin, handmade tofu is good, and good things take time," NaiNai says in her gentle voice.

And it takes cloth, from thread and fiber.

NaiNai turns on the heat and stirs slowly. A fresh, sweet smell fills my nose.

BUBBLE

BOBBLE

POPPLE

"Is it done? Is it done? Is it done?" I ask.
"Be patient, Lin," NaiNai says. "Tofu takes time."

And it takes heat and metal from
the sun and the earth.

I squeeze some lemon juice into the pot.

DRIP

DROP

PLOP

"Can I taste it?" I ask. I feel hungry.

"Look at how the soy milk curdles," NaiNai smiles. "It takes time for the chunks to form."

And it takes ingredients
to dance together.

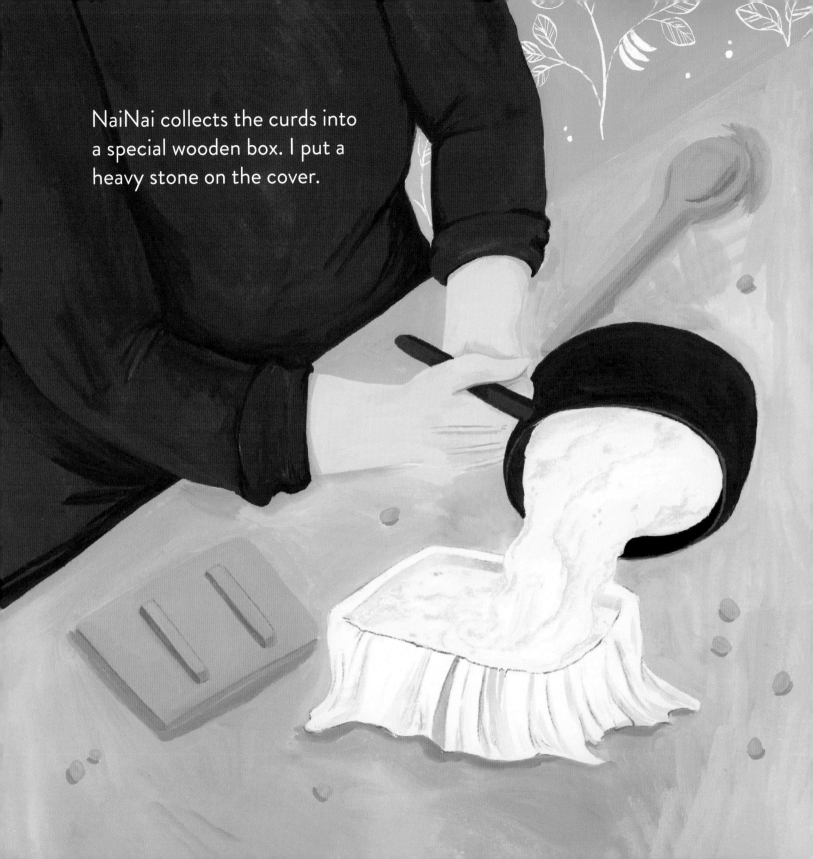

NaiNai collects the curds into a special wooden box. I put a heavy stone on the cover.

SQUEASE

SQUASH

SQUISH

"How much longer do I have to wait?" I sigh.

NaiNai says, "The curds take time to mold into shape."

And it takes some weight and space.

TICK

    TOCK

TICK

    TOCK

We wait
and wait
and wait.

"Can I have some now?" I ask.
"I'm so hungry!"

"Be patient," NaiNai says.
"Tofu takes a bit more time."

And it takes books, from stories and pictures.

"See? Now it looks like tofu!" NaiNai exclaims.

She takes the tofu out of the box and slices it into pieces. Then NaiNai puts tofu pieces, oil, soy sauce, and chopped green onions in a pan.

FRIZZLE

SIZZLE

HISS

Finally, it's ready.

Mama and Papa come home from work.

CHIT **CHAT** **CHIT** **CHAT**

Soon, we all sit around the table.

I take a bite.

Yummy!

Crispy outside
and tender inside.

I gobble it up.

Happiness fills my belly.

"This is delicious!" Mama says.

"I helped NaiNai make it!"
I say proudly.

"You must have been
so patient." Papa eats
one piece of tofu, and
another, and another.

Homemade tofu is the best!
I can't wait to make tofu again.

It just takes some time . . .

together with NaiNai.

More about Tofu

Tofu has been eaten in China for over 2,000 years! It has become a staple in many Asian countries, and the way it is made, how it tastes, and what people cook with it vary by region. The rest of the world was introduced to tofu in the early 1970s thanks to the increased interest in Buddhism and vegetarian lifestyles. Tofu is very high in protein and low in fat, so it is as healthy as it is tasty! It is a sustainable source of protein. That means it can be made without harming our planet, and it is the perfect plant-based alternative to animal proteins. Today, tofu has transformed from a typical Asian ingredient to one that is used and enjoyed all over the world.

Tofu comes in a few varieties based on density, ranging from silken to regular, firm, and extra firm. Silken tofu is the softest type and is commonly used in soup. It easily blends into things like custards and creams. Regular tofu works well for a crumbly scramble. The firmer varieties can be fried, sautéed, or baked into a chewy, meat-like protein.

Author's Note

This story's inspiration was born from my tofu-making experiences with my grandma. When I was a kid, I spent a lot of time with my grandparents in a small town in East China. Time after time, I sat by my grandma and watched her cooking, which included making tofu. She washed vegetables, chopped meat, stirred porridge, and cooked all the meals for the whole family. While cooking, my grandma always told me stories, which brought me to faraway places and times. After I moved to the US and had my own family, I began making tofu with my kids. They asked me a lot of questions about the process and all the tools we used. This reminded me of the sweet time I spent with my grandma in her small kitchen across the ocean. A story began to take shape.

Researching tofu recipes from around the world opened my eyes to so many dishes I didn't know about before—Korean soft tofu stew, Vietnamese fried tofu with tomato sauce, tofu tacos, tofish and chips, Indian butter tofu, vegan tofu kebab, and Chinese mapo tofu, just to name a few. It's easy to see that people all around the world love tofu! It inspired me to try tofu in global flavors and learn about the culture and history behind the different foods. A simple dish can truly connect us with the rest of the world.

Dear friends, what is your favorite dish? I can't wait to hear your stories.

For George and Kelsey, who truly taught me patience. –H.W.

For Monsieur Miguel. —J.J.

Text copyright © 2022 Helen H. Wu
Illustrations by Julie Jarema, copyright © 2022 Beaming Books

28 27 26 25 24 23 22   1 2 3 4 5 6 7 8 9

Hardcover ISBN: 978-1-5064-8035-0
Ebook ISBN: 978-1-5064-8150-0

Library of Congress Cataloging-in-Publication Data
Names: Wu, Helen H., author. | Jarema, Julie, illustrator.
Title: Tofu takes time / by Helen H. Wu, illustrated by Julie Jarema.
Description: Minneapolis, MN : Beaming Books, [2022] | Audience: Ages 3-8 |
Summary: "Lin makes tofu with her grandma and discovers that patience
brings a whole universe together in a simple dish made by a modern
Chinese American family"-- Provided by publisher.
Identifiers: LCCN 2021032638 (print) | LCCN 2021032639 (ebook) | ISBN
9781506480350 (hardcover) | ISBN 9781506481500 (ebook)
Subjects: CYAC: Chinese Americans--Fiction. | Cooking--Fiction. |
Grandmothers--Fiction. | Patience--Fiction.
Classification: LCC PZ7.1.W87 To 2022 (print) | LCC PZ7.1.W87 (ebook) |
DDC [E]--dc23
LC record available at https://lccn.loc.gov/2021032638
LC ebook record available at https://lccn.loc.gov/2021032639

VN0004589; 9781506480350; MAR2022

Beaming Books
PO Box 1209
Minneapolis, MN 55440
Beamingbooks.com